FIC FERMI
Fermine, Maxence
The black violin
R0019924287

MAY - - 2004

D1006302

The
BLACK
VIOLIN

Also by Maxence Fermine

Snow

The
BLACK
VIOLIN

A Novel

Maxence Fermine
Translation by Chris Mulhern

ATRIA BOOKS

New York London Toronto Sydney Singapore

ATRIA BOOKS

1230 Avenue of the Americas
New York, NY 10020

This book is a work of fiction. Names, characters, places and
incidents are products of the author's imagination or are used
fictitiously. Any resemblance to actual events or locales or
persons, living or dead, is entirely coincidental.

Copyright © 2000 by Arléa
English Language Translation Copyright © 2001
by acorn book company

Originally published in France in 2000 by Arléa
This translation first published by acorn book company,
England, 2003
Translated from the French by Chris Mulhern

All rights reserved, including the right to reproduce
this book or portions thereof in any form whatsoever.
For information address Editions Arléa, 16 rue de l'Odeon
75006 Paris, France

ISBN: 0-7434-5685-8

First Atria Books hardcover printing November 2003

10 9 8 7 6 5 4 3 2 1

ATRIA BOOKS is a trademark of Simon & Schuster, Inc.

For information regarding special discounts for bulk
purchases, please contact Simon & Schuster Special Sales
at 1-800-456-6798 or business@simonandschuster.com

Printed in the U.S.A.

The music is not in the notes, but in the silence between.

—WOLFGANG AMADEUS MOZART

R0019924287

The
BLACK
VIOLIN

PART
ONE

1

Johannes Karelsky was a violinist.

But in truth, he was far more than that.

For Johannes Karelsky was a genius.

And his secret wish was to write the most beautiful opera ever written.

2

In 1795, Johannes Karelsky was living in France, in the city of Paris. At thirty-one, he was at the height of his powers. And he still had another thirty-one years of life ahead of him. He was a virtuoso. He could play everything. Even those elaborate symphonies that audiences applaud rapturously, but which no one really understands.

Johannes's love for the violin was a passion that bordered on madness. He devoted every waking hour to his art. Every day, from dawn till dusk. Often he would become so absorbed that he would spend the whole day sitting with his eyes closed, lost within himself and his music.

3

Johannes's love for the violin began when he was only five years old.

One summer's morning, in the Tuileries gardens, a gypsy violinist had given him a glimpse of happiness, and had changed his life forever.

Johannes had been playing near a fountain when a man with dark hair and a beard appeared from the turning of a path. The stranger stopped, and squatting down, he lifted a violin from its case. The gypsy was so tall that the violin seemed like a toy in his hands. Intrigued by the man's appearance, a crowd soon began to gather around him, and Johannes was one of them.

Keeping time with his foot, the musician started with such a catchy tune that the child stared at him open-mouthed. Johannes was enthralled. He'd never heard music like this before.

The gypsy was no trained musician; in fact, he had only learned to play by ear, but each note he played came straight from his heart. It was a vibrant music, a music that told of the joys and sorrows of all the gypsies of the world. And they were feelings that Johannes shared, because young as he was, he could feel the voice of the violin within him.

The gypsy could see straightaway that Johannes was a kindred spirit. He looked into his eyes and began to play a polka—lyrical and beautiful, but with a melody so strange that no one else could follow it. But to Johannes, this was a revelation. For the first time, someone was speaking to him in a language that touched his heart. The language that would link him to the world forever.

As he listened more closely, Johannes began to realize that the gypsy was telling the story of his life. So the child closed his eyes and began to dream. . . .

He saw the ancient trackways that crossed Bohemia; he saw pine trees in the snow. He followed the endless wandering from one village to the next. He felt the cold, the hunger, and the loneliness. But he also saw faces flickering in the firelight and figures dancing, for despite all the hardship, there was laughter, and sometimes love.

When he had finished playing, the gypsy passed around the bowl, and the small metal pot clinked as a few coins were tossed in. When he came to Johannes, he crouched down in front of him and gently stroked his hair.

"And you, my little friend, have given me more with that look in your eyes than any of these ever could."

And with that, he was gone, as quickly as he had come.

From that day, Johannes knew he, too, was a musician.

Two years later, he had learned to play the violin.

4

Johannes had no actual teacher as such, although there were several who taught him the basics of the instrument. Soon, however, he was playing by himself, often not following any particular piece of music, but playing just for the simple pleasure of playing. It was clear that this child was no ordinary student. He imitated his teachers, and copied their technique, but already he was a great violinist, because the music he played came not from his hands but from his heart.

Johannes's teachers soon realized that there was nothing more they could teach him.

"There is no sense in continuing the lessons," one of them told his mother. "I cannot teach him what he already knows."

Madame Karelsky knew nothing about music, but she decided to trust his judgment. She had already lost both her husband and her fortune, and hoped that if what he said was true, her son's talent might even help to pay the rent.

And so, at the age of seven, Johannes Karelsky gave his first concert, in the church of Saint Louis-en-l'Île in Paris.

That night the church was crammed with people. Word of the young prodigy had spread and everyone wanted to hear him play.

The orchestra began the overture. And then, Johannes's turn came. When he made his appearance, standing there in his evening suit, his long black hair dangling on his shoulders, and his dreamy blue eyes, a murmur stirred the auditorium. On some faces one could read consternation; on a few there was even disappointment. The child seemed so frail. What kind of music could one expect from someone so young?

Holding the violin tight in one hand, Johannes took a few tentative steps forward and went to stand on the podium. He placed his instrument between his chin and his shoulder and began to play. Even from the first notes it was clear to everyone that he was no ordinary violinist.

While he was playing, the child closed his eyes and began to dance. And with each dip of the bow, each sway of the body, his confidence grew. Johannes and his violin became one. The notes flew from the violin, and rose pure and crystalline to the ancient stone vaulting of the ceiling. The audience was spellbound, amazed at his dazzling technique. The performance lasted only a matter of minutes, but throughout it, the air was taut with emotion.

As the final note faded away, there was a silence. A shiver ran through the auditorium. And then the clapping started.

After the concert many people rushed to congratulate the young violinist. Among the more enthusiastic were several famous musicians. One of them was so impressed that he went straight up to Madame Karelsky and offered then and there to take care of her son's career. At first, the mother pretended to refuse; she hesitated, he had to plead with her, but finally, almost reluctantly, she accepted.

More concerts followed. And within a few months, the young violinist had become a celebrity. In every salon in Paris, the same question was on everyone's lips:

"Who is this young prodigy? Who is Johannes Karelsky?"

His fame spread beyond the borders of France. Johannes was invited to Vienna, to Madrid, and to every royal palace in Europe. So, under the ever-watchful eye of his mother, the young violinist went from country to country, and everywhere he went he was a great success.

England was one of the first countries he visited, and he was given a tremendous reception there. His music seemed to break down the barriers that separated people, and for a while at least, they were able to forget the petty intrigues of politics. In London, his first performance created such a stir that his following seven concerts were completely sold out.

During a reception given in Johannes's honor, an English lady confided to Madame Karelsky:

"Your son is simply amazing! His friends must be so proud of him."

Madame Karelsky thanked her for the compliment, gave a slightly forced smile, and said:

"I don't really think my son has any friends."

The English lady seemed most surprised.

"But surely a young man of his age must have lots of friends?"

"Why don't you ask him for yourself?"

The English lady turned toward the child, who at that particular moment was listening to the tedious conversation of some young aristocrat, and asked him:

"Tell me, my child, who is your best friend?"

Johannes answered with no hesitation:

"My violin."

Each night, when the concert was over, Johannes became a child once again. He was known by everyone. But he had never felt so lonely.

5

His life of fame lasted ten years, until the death of his mother. When he lost her, Johannes lost the only thread that linked him to the world of reality. It was a loss he would feel for the rest of his life.

Tired of being paraded around every palace in Europe, Johannes decided to stop touring and settle in Paris, where he limited his performances to the occasional concert. He was seventeen, he still played beautifully, but he was no longer the sensation he had been.

Before long, everyone had forgotten about the child prodigy who had entertained royalty. These were troubled times, and there was talk of revolution. People scarcely had enough bread to eat, so music was the least of their worries.

Years went by. In order to make ends meet, Johannes spent his days giving violin lessons. And his evenings composing music.

All that mattered to him now was to dedicate himself to his true passion: to write an opera.

6

Johannes Karelsky would never have the chance to decide his future. In the spring of 1796, war decided it for him. He had just turned thirty-one.

He was living in a garret in Montmartre, and it was there, one morning in March, that Johannes was called up to join the army. Outside, a late fall of snow was silently drifting down. Time seemed to have come to a standstill.

The messenger tramped up the six floors of the building and stood, breathless, in front of the musician's door. He knocked loudly, and waited. Johannes opened the door and could see from his face that he was the bearer of bad tidings.

"It appears that the Motherland has need of your services," the messenger said, and handed him the letter. Johannes took the envelope and tore it open. His face paled as he read it.

"You're right," he said, "but what have I got to offer—except perhaps my life?"

The messenger smiled sympathetically.

A few minutes later, Johannes went down to the café, and found it full of other men who had also been called up. Some of them were impatient to follow the young twenty-eight-year-old general to whom Barras had assigned the Italian campaign. They drank a glass of absinthe together, then a second, then a third, all the while gazing at the low-cut blouse of the barmaid.

"To Bonaparte!" they cheered.

"To Bonaparte!"

"And to the great army on its way to Italy!"

Johannes didn't take part in the toasts. He just drank quietly, then said farewell to the others and went back home.

Back in his room, Johannes stared thoughtfully at the few possessions his mother had left him. Then he lay down on his bed, and in a haze of alcohol and sadness, he finally drifted to sleep.

By the time he woke up it was late afternoon, and night was falling on Paris. He stood at the window, watching. Here and there, lights began flickering. All was quiet.

Johannes took out his violin, ran some rosin over the bowstrings, and began to play. His thoughts were of the future, of the way his life was about to change. And the music that came from the violin was mournful and haunting.

The life he had known was over. War had seen to that. He had lost the chance to fulfill his dream. His opera would remain unfinished.

He was thirty-one years old, and there were many things he still wanted to do. But war had come.

7

Karelsky went south, to Nice, where Bonaparte was gathering his army. The shadow of war had loomed for many years now, and in the past, Johannes had always taken refuge in his art. This time, however, there was no escape.

This war would mean a forced march all the way to Vienna. But first they had to cross the Alps.

The army broke camp at dawn on the second of April 1796. The guns and their carriages began to move out. The Italian campaign had begun.

So here he was, going to Italy: the land where opera was born. Johannes was touched by the irony of his situation. He was a soldier now, and there'd be little time for music where he was going.

8

So this was war? The endless butchery and bloodshed, the dead and the dying all around him. These streams of ragged soldiers: unwashed, unfed, inhuman. And the constant deafening noise that hammered his eardrums until he was almost screaming out in pain.

What had become of the music that, not long ago, had soothed his spirit with the sound of a violin? The war had taken this, just as it had taken everything else.

But his war was to last only fourteen days. On the sixteenth of April, Johannes was wounded at the battle of Montenotte, and for him the war was over. While charging with the front line, Johannes had clashed with an Austrian Hussar, and the two men had run each other through with their swords. Clinging to Johannes's body, the Austrian had stared unbelieving into the eyes of the man he had just wounded. Then his gaze clouded over and he sank to his knees. The death rattle came from his throat, and Johannes fell to the ground beside him.

Some time later, the battle had ended and the clash of weapons had given way to silence.

When Johannes woke up it was dark, and a mist was beginning to settle on the field of battle. There were figures in the moonlight, furtive unsettling figures whose purpose he preferred not to contemplate, moving about the battlefield. Johannes wanted to get up but the pain in his groin was too great. The sword was still lodged inside him, its handle protruding from his stomach like a cross on a statue. On account of the intense cold, a clot of blood had formed over the wound and the bleeding had quickly ceased. But with the slightest movement, the sore would reopen and his life would drain away.

Johannes knew that his time had come. He looked once more at the carnage around him. The Austrian soldier lay only a few feet away, his hand still open as if making some desperate attempt to brandish a weapon he no longer held. His face twisted in a grotesque expression, defying death. To his right was a soldier who had been disemboweled, and beside him was his horse, lying dead on its side, its nostrils still wet from the chase. A little farther on, he saw yet another soldier dangling from a branch, his body broken by a cannonball. It was a landscape of smoke and ash. A landscape littered with ripped-open carts, and abandoned weapons, and mutilated bodies that had once been human.

The stretcher-bearers were making one final attempt to bring help to the wounded among so many dead. But all too often their cries drew no response from the men at their feet.

Johannes saw them coming closer. He tried to call out to them, but no sound would come from his mouth. His throat was so parched that his tongue felt like a dry stone washed in blood.

The stretcher-bearers went away and the silence fell once again.

Johannes looked at the moon for one last time, he saw the sword handle glinting in the darkness above him, and then he closed his eyes.

He was woken by a sudden rustling in the air, the sound of a cloth flapping in the wind.

Was it the wind? The wind in the tunic of the soldier lying next to him? Or was this what the coming of death was like?

He opened his eyes to find a woman standing over him. She was dressed in a long black cavalry cape and was holding the bridle of a black horse. Johannes could feel her looking at him intently, her eyes bright in the darkness.

How could she have reached him without making a sound, apart from that faint flapping of her cloak that had revealed her presence? It seemed to Johannes that there was something otherworldly about her.

The stranger stood there, motionless. Apparently just contemplating the dying man.

Johannes shivered with fear, but realized there was nothing he could do. It was too late to do anything now. He watched her tying the reins of her mount to a tree. She took a flask from the saddle and, kneeling beside him, she cupped his head in her hands and helped him to drink. And then, in that desolate landscape, she began to sing. Her voice was so pure, so enchanting, that Johannes forgot his wounds and found himself drifting to a place where the pain could not reach him.

All night she held him cradled in her arms, and all night she sang. And when at last it began to get light, she kissed him; and as their lips touched, Johannes closed his eyes and fell asleep.

9

When Johannes woke up, a medical officer was dressing his wounds, breathing wafts of garlic and stale tobacco into his face.

The doctor was talking with one of his superiors whose profile flickered in the lamplight.

"Tell me, Doctor, is this man out of danger yet?"

"In a way, sir, yes he is. For him the war is over, and he'll be remembered as a hero . . . because he'll be dead before daybreak."

Johannes grabbed the doctor's arm and, with his last strength, he pleaded:

"Please give me something! I want to die now! Why let me go on suffering like this?"

The doctor took his hand and tried to calm him down.

"Don't waste your breath, young man. You'll be dead soon enough, I promise you that."

"I want to go to sleep and never wake up again. Listen to me, tell the general I won't fight anymore. Tell Bonaparte I'm dead!"

The doctor wiped Johannes's forehead, then he raised his head and looked at the officer who was standing in front of him, beseeching him with his eyes to say a few words of comfort.

The general looked down at the wounded man and regarded him coldly.

"Be brave!" he said. "Face death as you would any mortal enemy!"

But Johannes had fainted, and would never hear what Bonaparte had told him.

10

Johannes Karelsky did not become a hero. And neither did he die.

When he came to, the following day, the pain had subsided a little. And the day after that it became clear he would survive.

He was sent back to join the wounded behind the lines. His convalescence would take several months, and in the meantime, there was nothing he could do but wait. Little by little, he began to regain his strength. Though deep in his heart was a wound that even time would never heal.

The Italian campaign was going well. In battle after battle, the enemy was suffering heavy losses. The advance pushed on, relentless. Each day more wounded were brought in, and each day the rumble of cannons could be heard from afar.

Sometimes, in the evening, Johannes would take his violin and play for his fellow soldiers. He played especially for the wounded and the dying. From time to time, the priest would come and fetch him to ease the pains of some dying man. But there were times when even music could do little. For the suffering was simply too great.

One evening, Johannes decided to accompany the stretcher-bearers on to the battlefield. He sat on a moonlit hilltop and played his violin for the wounded who lay there. He began to wonder if even the dead might somehow be able to hear his music as it drifted across the darkening field.

When he had fully recovered he was sent to rejoin his unit. He found himself back once again among soldiers. Soldiers whose bodies were tough and strong, but whose minds had been scarred by the horrors of the war.

That first night, in his tent, he took up his violin and played. His companions glared at him.

The war sounded very different to them. Their hearts had been hardened by the shriek of shells and the thunder of cannons. Tenderness was something they remembered, but were no longer capable of feeling.

"Stop it!" shouted one of them. "You'll end up reducing us all to tears with that thing. Why don't you learn to play the trumpet instead!"

The bow stopped in midair before closing on the strings and smothering their resonance. Without a word, Karelsky went to lie down on his cot.

When he woke up he found his violin by his bed. It was broken. A tangle of strings and splintered wood. He never discovered who had done it.

He never talked about it, nor did he try to find out who was to blame. For Johannes knew that whoever it was, the war would claim him in the end. And leave him twisted and broken. Just like his violin.

11

When the French army entered Venice, on the sixteenth of May 1797, it was as if someone had cast a spell of silence over the whole city. The men were frozen in their tracks, their cries crystallized by its beauty and stillness. Johannes was struck by the tranquillity emanating from each tiny street, a tranquillity he had not experienced for a long time.

For eleven centuries, the Serenissima Republic had withstood the threat of barbarian invasion. Secure in its mastery of the waves, it had ruled over an empire that extended all the way to the Orient. Now that empire had disappeared, wiped from the map as if it had never even existed, and an army was waiting at the gates.

"Venice is more than a city," said Johannes to the medical officer standing beside him, "it is a dream stretching out into the sea."

And as he watched the lines of exhausted men tramping past so much gold, so many ancient buildings and ornate monuments, what he saw was as unreal as any dream.

Johannes stood there, listening to the silence.

"Venice," he whispered to himself. "It is even more beautiful than I'd imagined it."

The city seemed to float upon the waters of the lagoon, like some magnificent galleon. It was indeed very beautiful. And yet, even as he spoke, it was sinking, and one day, it would disappear forever.

Venice was a city of paintings and palaces, overflowing with gold and with jewels. A city of silence, and water. In the space of a few days, the army had plundered the gold, the jewels, and the paintings. It had taken over the palaces and violated the silence. Then it continued its march across Europe.

Bonaparte was well aware of the price

Hannibal had paid for letting his army linger in Capua, and was already advancing on Vienna.

The army left behind only a small occupying force. And having been wounded in battle, Johannes Karelsky was one of them.

He was to spend the next six months in this, the most silent of all cities. The ideal place to return to his music. The ideal place to begin work on his opera.

12

He was billeted with an old man who owned a crumbling mansion, not far from Piazza San Marco.

When Johannes introduced himself, showing his billeting card, he realized that the war wasn't the same for everyone.

"Johannes Karelsky. Pleased to meet you."

"My name is Erasmus. What can I do for you?"

"I am a French soldier. I shall be living here whilst I'm in Venice."

The old man made no reply.

"I have no wish to cause you any trouble,"

Johannes went on. "I shall be as quiet as I can and try not to disturb you."

Erasmus smiled. It was a small, shy smile. But it was enough to reassure Johannes.

"I appreciate your kindness, sir. I myself am too old to care much about this war. Obviously I've heard of Bonaparte and, if Venice has now become French, then there is not much I can do about it."

The old man spoke good French. He stepped to one side to allow Karelsky to enter. Johannes nodded his thanks and went in.

"Where did you learn to speak our language, sir?"

"In Paris," he said, "many years ago."

"And what were you doing in Paris, if I may ask?"

"I was working there. I'm a violin-maker, I make violins."

Johannes looked at him, curiously.

"A violin-maker, you said?"

"That's right. Why, what of it?"

"Nothing. But I have a feeling that fate may have brought us together."

13

There were many musical souls adrift on that raft of silence that is Venice.

There was the music of Johannes Karelsky.

There was the music of Erasmus, the violin-maker.

And there was the music of the war.

But of that, the two men never spoke.

Each morning, Johannes would leave the violin-maker's house and report to his garrison. Each morning was the same. He was bored to tears. Most of the time he sat around doing nothing. Occasionally there were a few forms to fill in. And he found that even more tedious.

On Pentecost day, the fourth of June, a magnificent pageant was held in Piazza San Marco. Soldiers of both the French and Italian armies took part in the celebrations. The Venetian flags were lowered, and the tricolor of the French Republic was raised. At the end of the ceremony the Golden Book was burnt, together with all the other symbols of the Doge's power.

In the evening, a new opera was premiered at the Fenice. The stage was draped with silks and banners. Under the heel of its new ruler, Venice was making a great show of happiness.

Johannes was obliged to take part in the ceremony, though he had no taste for it. He was sick of the war, of its horrors and excesses. So having done his duty, he refused to get drunk with the other soldiers but instead went back to Erasmus's house. The old man was bent over his workbench, carefully polishing the back of a violin.

"So being French, or Austrian, or Italian makes no difference to you?" asked Johannes.

"My real homeland is music. I don't care that much about the rest. Although being a soldier you wouldn't understand that."

Johannes shook his head and sighed. "I was forced to become a soldier. But before that I was a musician."

Erasmus was taken aback. He stared at Johannes, a frown wrinkling his forehead:

"What instrument do you play?"

There was a long silence, during which the violin-maker went back to his polishing. And then Johannes replied:

"The violin."

Erasmus stopped. He stared at the younger man intently for a few moments. Then, deciding that he was probably telling the truth, he took down a violin that was hanging up above his workbench, and handed it over.

"Show me," he said.

Johannes had not played for several months, and the violin felt strangely light in his hands. He brought it up to his nose, and sniffed at the wood. Then he stroked it slowly, as if he were caressing a woman. And settling the violin between his shoulder and chin, he took up the bow and began to play. He played slowly at first, but gradually increased his tempo, dashing off a series of dazzling pizzicati. He stopped abruptly and stood still for a while, his eyes closed, quivering with pleasure.

He opened his eyes, to find that the old man was looking at him. For a while he just stared. Then he grinned and said:

"Welcome to the land of music! Welcome to the home of Erasmus!"

14

The home of Erasmus the violin-maker was, without a doubt, one of the oldest and most dilapidated of all the houses in Venice. But it also had more atmosphere than most. It was in a tiny street, below the level of the lagoon, and would therefore be one of the first to disappear when Venice finally sinks beneath the waters.

Erasmus led a simple life. His needs were few. In fact, apart from music, he needed hardly anything at all. But he soon began to enjoy having Johannes's company.

Erasmus had three precious possessions: a chessboard, which he believed to be magic; an ageless bottle of grappa; and a black violin. The old man also had three special talents: He was the finest violin-maker in Venice, he never lost a game of chess, and he was the maker of the most exceptional grappa in Italy. He made the latter in a still he had installed in a small room at the back of his workshop. And that was how he spent his days: In the mornings he would be found repairing or making violins, in the afternoon he distilled his grappa, and in the evenings he would play chess. And thus, the whole day passed, every moment of it dedicated to one or other of his passions. He was always doing something. Something related to either music, or drinks, or chess.

When he drank, Erasmus would talk incessantly. When he wasn't talking about violins, he would talk about grappa. When he wasn't talking about grappa, he would talk about chess. When he wasn't talking about chess, he would talk about music. And when he wasn't talking about music, he wouldn't talk at all.

It was there, in the workshop of the old man

who had now become his friend that, night after night, during a never-ending game of chess, Johannes finally found the inspiration he needed to compose his opera.

15

"So tell me," Johannes asked his friend one night, "what's so interesting about the distillation of grappa?"

"Interesting? It's intoxicating!" answered Erasmus.

On the chessboard the black bishop was protecting the queen.

"In order to obtain a quality grappa, both love and time are needed."

Johannes lifted his head and looked up at the old man.

"Love and time . . ." he repeated.

Then he moved his knight without realizing

that this left his king completely unprotected. Erasmus checked him. Three moves later, it was checkmate.

"And how much love and time is needed?"

"Neither too much, nor too little. It varies depending on the year. Checkmate!"

Erasmus stood up, took two glasses, filled them with the honey-colored liquor, and handed one to the violinist.

"Taste this, Johannes! The first sip is like fire! The second, like velvet! And the third . . . like a dream, beginning!"

Karelsky took exactly three sips, swallowing each one, slowly. The violin-maker watched him with a paternal gaze.

"Time," said Erasmus sadly, "that's something I haven't got much of left. . . . Love, well . . ."

He pursed his lips, made a face, and gave a long sigh.

16

"What about chess?" Johannes asked him the following evening. "What makes that so interesting?"

"Interesting? It's fascinating! To become a good chess player you need a touch of madness about you. You need to picture in your mind the chessboard with all its sixty-four black and white squares, and you need to repeat this again and again until you begin to lose your mind. In fact it's the only game that relies on madness. And that's precisely the reason I play it, and love it."

"I don't think I'm quite mad enough for this game."

"Oh, I promise you that if every night you play against an imaginary opponent—as I've been doing for the last fifty-four years—you'll get there in the end."

To tell the truth, Johannes was not that interested in grappa or chess. But he would talk about either, just to please the old man. Music, on the other hand, was a subject that fascinated him. And the black violin that was hanging above the old man's workbench intrigued him. He had never seen a violin like it. It was so black, so sleek, so beautiful. And yet, there was something rather unsettling about it. It had a presence that made it seem almost alive.

17

"What about that black violin?" Johannes asked him the third evening. "What's interesting about that?"

Erasmus looked up and paled slightly.

"That violin? If I were you I wouldn't even touch one of its strings."

"Why? Is it so bad that it's not worth playing?"

"Quite the opposite! It's the most extraordinary instrument I've ever come across. A mere breath is enough to set it vibrating. But the music it makes is so strange, that to hear it once is to be changed forever. It is like taking a draught of pure happiness. Once you have tasted it, you are never the same again. Playing the black violin is like that, too."

"Have you ever played it?"

"Only once. A long time ago. I haven't touched it since. It is like love. When you have been in love—and I'm talking here about true love—it is something you can never forget. There is nothing worse than having been truly happy once in your life. From that moment on, everything makes you sad, even the most insignificant things."

18

That night in his room, Johannes worked on his opera for a while. Then he fell asleep and dreamt about the black violin.

When he got up the next day, he glanced briefly at his manuscript book, lying where he'd left it beside his bed. And he noticed a very strange thing: It was empty. There was nothing written in it. All his work had somehow disappeared during the night.

Johannes was baffled. In his mind he went back over the conversation he'd had the previous evening and the dream he had during the night. It was all very strange. Perhaps he had dreamt the whole thing. Perhaps he had never actually written anything down in the first place. And yet, that didn't make sense. In fact, the more he thought about it, the less sense it made.

During the day he tried to take his mind off things by concentrating on the dull tasks to which his duty bound him. But in the evening when he got back, the first thing that caught his eye was the black violin hanging there on the wall. He had the strange suspicion that the black violin had something to do with what had happened.

19

A few days later, Johannes was talking to Erasmus about his art, and about the music that he could feel within himself but couldn't, for some mysterious reason, write down on paper. To his surprise, the old man said:

"So, tell me. When will I be allowed to listen to this famous opera you are always talking about?"

Johannes was so taken aback that he couldn't reply. It was the first time Erasmus had shown any interest in his music. In fact, most of the time, whenever Johannes was talking, the old man would simply nod his head, and the young violinist had begun to think that Erasmus wasn't really listening to him at all.

Erasmus repeated his question:

"Anyway, this opera—when's it going to be finished then?"

"It's too early to say. A couple of months, maybe. If everything goes well."

Two months passed and the old man asked him again.

"So, how long is this opera going to be? How many pages?"

Johannes found himself saying:

"One hundred and sixty-seven."

"How many notes is that?"

"Oh, seventeen thousand, six hundred . . . and twenty-three—that's not counting the pauses."

"And how much have you written?"

Johannes didn't reply. For the fact was that the more time he spent composing his opera, the more imaginary it had become.

20

Johannes was reluctant to tell the old man the truth.

But one night, he could wait no longer. He had tried seven times to fill the manuscript book. And seven times his opera had disappeared.

The two men were sitting at the table, eating a fine roasted pheasant accompanied by a good bottle of red wine. It was the beginning of October. Each day, the sun disappeared a little earlier into the lagoon. Erasmus and Johannes weren't celebrating anything in particular, just the passing of summer and the arrival of the first frost. The wine was fragrant and full-bodied, and brought a feeling of warmth and well-being, like the memory of the season that would soon be gone forever.

The time had come for Johannes to speak with his friend.

But Erasmus beat him to it.

"I have the feeling that there is something you wish to tell me."

Johannes stared into his plate for a long time before replying:

"How did you guess?"

In that moment the two men were so close that even in silence, they could share all that they needed to say.

"It's obvious. You've been looking upset for a while now. Tell me what's bothering you."

Johannes took a sip of wine, then told the old man about his music book.

"You must have dreamt it, Johannes. That kind of thing only happens in dreams."

"No, believe me. There must be something that is stopping me from writing."

"Like a spell?"

Johannes was about to mention the black violin but, at the last minute, changed his mind.

"Perhaps . . ."

Even as he spoke, he could feel the presence of the black violin.

"Well, in that case, it's better to wait." And with that, Erasmus left the table and went to sit in his old armchair.

He stared intently at the chessboard, where the black knight was protecting his queen. Johannes sat down opposite the old man. Erasmus took the grappa bottle, and the two men resumed the game they had left the night before.

"Wait for what?"

"For whatever has to happen—to happen."

"I don't understand."

"It's all about hope. One day, you will write your opera. And you will play it. Perhaps only once. Perhaps only to yourself. But play it, you will. Of that I am certain. No happiness in this world is possible without hope."

Johannes slowly repeated the words the old man had just spoken.

". . . no happiness in this world. . . . But happiness is possible in dreams!" Then he said, "I've never told you this before, but that night I was wounded, while I was lying there on the battle-field, a mysterious woman came to me. She may have been an apparition, or she may have been a dream, but since then I have thought about her every night."

Erasmus became thoughtful for a moment.

"Wait for your dream to become reality. And then you will be free. It will happen, sooner or later. All you have to do is wait.'

"But wait for how long?"

"It is not a matter of time, be it minutes or years, it is always worth waiting."

"Always?" asked Johannes.

"Always." Erasmus nodded.

Johannes paused, his hand hovering over the black queen.

"I don't know if I can be that patient," he said.

But for the time being, he decided to wait.

21

The following evening, while playing the same game of chess that they abandoned every night, the old man leaned forward, and said:

"I've been thinking, Johannes . . . that opera of yours, you can't just write it, you need to live it first."

"I'd never thought of that. To be honest, I'd never really thought there was much point to everyday life."

"Ah, but I have an idea that may make you change your mind."

"Really? And what would that be then?"

"You must begin by looking for the next part of your dream."

"And where might I find that?"

"Well, there's a part of it everywhere. But most of all, it is within you."

Johannes raised his eyebrows. Then, without really thinking, he picked up his bishop and slid it back along the diagonal.

"Every soul wanders the path of its own dreams. And you, dreaming about that mysterious woman, are a case in point."

"But dreams are like that. In dreams there are no boundaries. That's what's beautiful about them, isn't it?"

"Of course, in a dream, anything is possible."

"Well, what's that got to do with everyday life?"

Erasmus didn't answer immediately. He stared at the chessboard for a long time. Then he took Johannes's bishop with his queen. He took a big gulp of grappa and turned his gaze toward the black violin that was hanging on the wall. Finally, turning to face Johannes, he said:

"You see, Johannes . . . dreams are only finished—by being broken."

22

One Sunday, in the month of November 1797, while the snow was falling on Venice, Johannes went to San Zaccaria for vespers. When the service was over the congregation got up and began to file out, but Johannes stayed behind.

As he knelt there alone in the House of God, he heard someone singing. It was a woman's voice, and the song she sang had a frail, tragic beauty. Johannes felt a shiver down his spine. It was the same voice he had heard that night on the battlefield.

Johannes was overcome with happiness. He

did not dare open his eyes, fearing that if he did so, the spell would disappear and the song would come to an end. He needed it to go on a little longer. He was waiting, waiting for something to form and grow inside him. Like a birth, like the coming into this world of a part of his soul. For this was the voice for the opera he was writing. And that opera was destined to be sung by this voice.

When the song ended, Johannes opened his eyes. Slowly, he stood up and looked around him. But there was no one there. The music and the voice had gone, leaving only the emptiness of the church.

He was alone. With the memory of a voice echoing around him.

For the second time, he had found her, and lost her.

23

When Johannes told Erasmus about the voice he had heard, he saw a light twinkling in the old man's eyes.

"So you have met her at last?"

Johannes had no idea what to say.

"Do you know who she is?" asked Erasmus. "Do you know whom that voice belongs to?"

Silence.

"I thought so . . ."

The two men were staring at the same spot on the wall.

"Sit down, Johannes. I have something to tell you."

Johannes sat down and, while Erasmus was pouring him a drink, he realized that he was about to hear the secret of the black violin.

PART
TWO

24

My love for the violin was a passion that bordered on madness. I wanted to be known as Erasmus, the greatest violin-maker of all time. I knew even then I had what it took. I knew I was a genius.

At the time this story begins, I was only a boy. I was living a long way from Venice, in the city of Cremona, the very birthplace of the violin. It was in Cremona that the first violin was made at the beginning of the sixteenth century. And it was there that I learned my art.

My parents had always wanted me to become a violin-maker, but my own aspirations were greater still. I wanted to make the finest violin that had ever been made. A violin so perfect, with a sound so sublime, that whoever played it would touch the heavens, and speak to God himself.

25

From my earliest days, I have loved and lived for music. I have tried to serve God with the gift he gave me. For without being arrogant, I always knew I had a special gift, and the willpower to practice it. Not to mention that hint of madness that can make a man a genius or a madman—which, as we both know, can amount to much the same thing in the end.

I devoted every waking hour to perfecting my art. I woke, ate, slept, and lived only for music. The music I was trying to catch, and seal forever inside my violins.

To tell you the truth, that perfect music was in fact a human voice. The voice of a woman. A voice I knew even better than my own. But a voice I could hear only in my dreams.

26

In my opinion, no instrument resembles the human voice as closely as the violin. From the very first time I heard the strings of a violin set quivering by the touch of a bow, I fell in love. And my passion has never waned.

When I was only a very small boy my father played me a piece of music that I found deeply moving.

"I'd like to do that one day," I said when the piece came to an end.

"What—you'd like to become a violinist?"

"No, not exactly. I would like to make violins

that can touch a person's heart. I'd like to make the finest violin ever made!"

My father raised an eyebrow.

"And you're sure that's what you'd really like to do?"

"Yes," I said at once.

"Very well, then."

The following day he took me to the workshop of Francesco Stradivari. His father Antonio, the great Stradivarius, had recently passed away.

27

Francesco Stradivari was a gifted craftsman, but he lacked the genius of his more famous father. At the time he took me on as his apprentice, the family business was already falling into decline. And Francesco himself had only a year left to live. The golden age of Cremona's violin-making was drawing to a close.

Francesco was a man of few words, and the only way he had to express his joys and his sorrows was through music. He spent so much of his time playing that he ended up leaving the violin-making almost entirely in the hands of his apprentices. All he did was to put his name on them when they were finished, or when someone famous ordered one, the name of his father.

In those days, anybody who was anybody wanted to own a Stradivarius. Indeed, some musicians refused to play any other kind of violin. And no court orchestra was considered complete unless it had at least a couple of the master's violins. So the kings, the princes, and the dukes were prepared to spend vast amounts of money just to be able to say that the violins their orchestra played had been signed by the famous violinmaker.

One day, the King of Sweden sent a messenger to Francesco to commission a small viola as a gift to his son. The messenger told him the King wanted a Stradivarius. But the instruments made by the master had all been sold, and there wasn't a single one left in the workshop. So for a very reasonable price, Francesco gave him an instrument he had just made himself. On the back of the viola was a small plaque that read:

FRANCISCUS STRADIVARIUS CREMONENSIS
FILIUS ANTONII FACEBAT ANNO 1742

Two months later, the King's messenger returned to Cremona.

"His Majesty the King of Sweden is furious. The viola he purchased is not a real Stradivarius."

He took a bag of gold out of his pocket and threw it down on the table.

"His Majesty trusts that this extra is sufficient to purchase the real thing."

Francesco snatched the viola. "A real Stradivarius, eh?" he hissed between his teeth. "I'll get you one straightaway!"

He went to his workshop and closed the door. He could be heard clattering about inside for a few minutes. When he returned, he was carrying an instrument that appeared to be almost identical to the one before. Only this time, the plaque read:

ANTONIUS STRADIVARIUS CREMONENSIS
FACEBAT ANNO 1737

The King of Sweden began to spread the rumor that he had paid a small fortune to buy the very last masterpiece to have been made by the master of Cremona.

Francesco had obviously just changed the small plaque on the back of the viola, but by doing so, he had doubled its value.

Thanks to the King of Sweden, Francesco became a very wealthy man. But as his wealth grew, so did his bitterness.

By this stage, it was clear that he regarded himself as a failure, witnessing the last days of a dying art slipping away. His father's fame cast such a shadow over him, that he no longer gained any satisfaction from practicing his art. He soon tired altogether of the business of making violins, and was content to simply oversee the work of his apprentices.

In the morning he would warm up his fingers by playing a few quick arpeggios. Then he would move on to something more demanding, and finally, in the evening, he would play something he had composed himself.

If one of his apprentices dared to interrupt by asking him a question, Francesco Stradivari would simply go on playing till he could see anxiety growing in his apprentice's eyes. At that point he would pause in his performance and say:

"When the music you play is able to move

someone to the point of tears, you will realize that your voice is a waste of breath."

He was all too aware of the fact that he was just the son of the greatest violin-maker who had ever lived. And this he found extremely humiliating.

In contrast to my silent master, I was an exuberant young man, much given to expressing the music I had within me by endless chattering, shouts, and laughter. For while Francesco tended toward silence, I drew sound like a sponge.

Music could have no better instrument than my passion for the violin. A passion akin to that of the great Stradivarius. A man I had never actually met but whom I was sure I understood better than anyone else.

28

Many years after the death of Antonio Stradivari, his workshop still radiated the great violin-maker's extraordinary energy.

Some people couldn't feel it at all, but each time I entered the master's workshop I felt his presence as strong as ever. In that jumble of bits of wood, and harmonic tables, and of instruments in various stages and states of repair, amid all that clutter, Francesco could see only the raw materials destined to become a musical instrument. But for me it was always far more than that. For in that "clutter" I could discern the beginnings of a miracle. A miracle that could produce the only sound that could link the world of man to the world of the angels.

29

The story of the black violin begins with a dream.

I was always a bit of a dreamer. I'd daydream while I was at work in the Stradivaris' workshop, and I'd dream in my bed at night. In fact, besides making violins, the time I spent in my dreams was the happiest part of my existence.

And each night, the dream was the same.

I saw a woman walking toward me. I knew nothing about her, not even her face or the shape of her body. But her golden voice filled my nights and would break my heart each time I heard it.

The truth was that I had fallen in love with a woman who didn't exist.

Night after night I would find myself back in that dream; I'd be walking around a strange town. From somewhere far off came the sound of a violin, and turning into one of the small alleys, I'd begin walking toward it. I would wander the deserted, moonlit streets, until I came to a stone bridge crossing a canal. I could see the reflection of a masked face in the still water. And there, standing in the middle of the bridge, was a woman playing the violin. She had her back to me. I would approach her very slowly and touch her gently on the shoulder. The young woman would turn to face me and I would discover that she wasn't playing the violin. She was the violin! Her body was smooth and curved in the shape of a violin, and her voice was its sound. She held a sheet of music in her hands, and the aria she was singing was welling up from within her like some celestial music. At that point, the woman would open her arms, and as I stepped forward to embrace her, everything—the woman, the music, and the dream—would all be engulfed in a sea of flames. And I would wake up.

Each time I made a violin I was trying to re-create the sound of her voice, but try as I might, I could never succeed.

The dream was my secret. I never told a soul. Neither Francesco Stradivari nor my fellow apprentices in the workshop. Nobody knew but me.

30

In 1743 Francesco died, and with him the famous Stradivari family came to an end.

My fellow apprentices left Cremona and went to other cities in Europe. I found myself alone in the workshop. The business was failing.

One day, the Count of Ferenzi arrived at the door. He was passing through Cremona on his way back to Venice and wished to commission a violin. He was a disconcerting character, accustomed to giving orders, and evidently very rich. He was traveling in a sumptuous carriage, accompanied by two servants. He explained that he had urgent business to attend to and had to return to Venice at once. He therefore had no time to waste in small talk.

"I want you to make a violin. I want nothing but the best. And I want it delivered on the first Sunday of October."

"Sir, that gives me very little time to honor your . . ."

"There may be little time, but the reward will be substantial. You may name your price and whatever it is, I shall pay."

I considered his words for a moment and soon reached the conclusion that I didn't really have much choice. More to the point, I felt I had served my apprenticeship well and was now anxious to undertake a commission of my own.

"Very well," I said. "I shall work both night and day to have the violin ready in time, and when it is finished, I will come to Venice to deliver it myself."

The Count paid me and left.

I shut myself in the workshop and set to work immediately.

I decided to base the violin on a model designed by Antonio Stradivari. The master's design followed complex rules, which I had to study for some time before getting down to work.

First I made the body of the instrument. Then, having tested its acoustic qualities, which I found to be excellent, I went on to the varnishing stage. Finally I added the strings. Then I tried it out, and that was the moment I realized I had finally become a master violin-maker.

I had not slept much over the last few weeks, but within the short space of time I'd been given, I had succeeded in crafting a violin of which anyone would be proud.

At dawn on the first Sunday of October, I set off for Venice.

31

I was twenty years old, and was seeing Venice for the very first time. I was seeing it as I would never see it again. Untouched by memory or regret.

I entered the city with two things that were pure and beautiful. One was my heart. The other, a violin.

And little did I know that I was about to lose both. Forever.

32

As I came into the city, I was amazed by the feeling of lightness that filled my whole body. I felt a thrill of excitement, a sudden feeling of joy and well-being. This was the place to fall in love.

It was the beginning of autumn. The Carnival season had just started, and people were happy. For the next six months, until the coming of Lent, Venice would be a place of celebration.

I had arrived by boat and disembarked alongside the Ferenzi Palace. It was a beautiful two-story Venetian mansion, its entrance facing the Grand Canal. The imposing ochre façade was reflected in the dark water, although I noticed that here and there, the paintwork was flaking off to reveal the plaster beneath. I went up the steps and rang the bell. A valet dressed in full livery opened the door.

"My name is Erasmus and I'm looking for the Count of Ferenzi. I have a violin to deliver to him."

"If you would be so kind as to wait here for a moment, I shall inform the Count of your arrival," and with that, he disappeared up the stairs.

I found myself in a large hall. While he was away, I looked around the room. The floor was tiled in black and white like a chessboard. Several paintings, many of which showed the lagoon in the various seasons of the year, were hanging from the walls. Statues of naked women stood coyly inside niches. The tall arched windows offered views of the Grand Canal, slightly misted by the morning dew. At the bottom of the stairs, I noticed a beautiful shelf of pink marble with a silver tobacco box resting on it. I marveled at what I saw, realizing that these were only a taste of the riches that must lie within the palace itself. And yet, like the rest of Venice, the Ferenzi

Palace was resting on stilts that were sinking slowly into the silt of the lagoon, and nothing, not all the gold in the world, could do anything about it. The city was doing its best to hide behind an elegant façade, for it still wanted to be seen as imposing and powerful, when in fact all it had left were the memories of bygone days. I noticed that the wall leading up the stairs was cracked in places, and that beneath its veneer of ancient splendor it could no longer hide the effects of time.

In due course, the Count himself appeared. He looked at me curiously, as if he'd never seen me before. It was clear that the years had taken their toll on him, too.

"I understand that you have come to see me. What can I do for you?"

"My name is Erasmus. I have brought the violin you commissioned."

"Oh yes, I remember now. It's not actually for me, it is for my daughter, Carla. I wanted to give it to her for her birthday, which incidentally coincides with the beginning of the Carnival. I never know what to buy her. . . . Every year I have the same problem. She already has everything!

But this time I think I have chosen something truly original."

Then, in a lower tone, as if imparting a great secret, he said:

"My daughter is not here at the moment. She will not be returning until this evening. I would like you to present the violin to her personally. I myself have to leave right away for Verona, where I have urgent business to attend to. Unfortunately I shall be away for a while. Ah yes, and may I make one further request?"

"Most certainly."

"Very well. Come back this evening. I am giving a fancy dress ball to celebrate the beginning of the Carnival. If you would be so kind as to attend, you could present the violin to Carla on my behalf. I really would be most grateful."

"It will be a pleasure, sir."

He thanked me and, as if he were talking to himself, he added:

"This wretched business really is most inconvenient. My daughter is singing at the Fenice tomorrow night, and I would so much have liked to have seen her."

"Your daughter is a singer?"

"Well, not exactly. You see, I've hired out the Fenice for her. Why don't you go along yourself. She is a soprano. They say she has a golden voice! When you have listened to her once, you will never be able to forget her."

I promised to do as he suggested.

"Very good, very good. Now if you will excuse me, I have things to attend to. Good-bye to you, sir."

And with that, he left me.

33

I walked around Venice 'til the evening. The festivities were just beginning. One could feel a spirit of anticipation in the air, a hint of frivolity.

I had lunch at a trattoria near Campo Sant'Angelo, dining on cuttlefish cooked in its ink.

In the late afternoon I wandered around the small streets and bridges, going nowhere in particular, happy just to lose myself in the charms of the city.

A group of courtesans passed me, dressed in long black capes, wearing white masks and carrying tridents; they turned around to look at me and laughed at the way I was dressed. Irritated by their teasing, I decided it was time to get dressed up myself, and went to a costume-maker to choose something to wear.

I emerged a short while later, feeling very proud of my new outfit. In the center of town the festivities were now in full flow, and I found myself surrounded by masks, jugglers, acrobats, and musicians of all kinds.

The carnival season was opened officially with a shower of confetti and streamers. A fire-eater performed by the lagoon, and he in turn was followed by a troupe of clowns.

I fell in with the procession, and even exchanged a few words with complete strangers. Beneath the mask, you had no idea who you were talking to. Whether they were a duchess or a servant girl, or even whether they were a man or a woman? Behind my mask I could have been anyone, too. A duke, or a dignitary, or even the Doge himself. Perhaps even a spy or some fearsome brigand.

On entering this city I had plunged headlong into the spirit of Carnival. I had left the real world behind, and from now on, anything was possible.

A group of dice players was squatting on the corner of a street. One of them had a pile of coins, which he was keeping close to him. His companions were frowning, hoping their luck would change as they risked their few remaining coins on one last throw of the dice. Sitting on the handrail of one of the bridges, some masked figures were making bawdy comments at the passersby. A couple of playful gondoliers tried to cajole me into giving them money by telling me jokes. A tightrope walker dressed all in white was walking a rope stretched over the water. On a street corner some flute music drew my attention, and an insistent Pulcinella took me by the hand and spun me around. The city was one enormous stage where a dreamlike fantasy was being played out.

Soon it was nightfall. The canals grew darker, and the moonlight was reflected in their ink-black water. The narrow streets were emptying out while the palaces started to light up one by one. The air grew colder; the time had come to continue the festivities inside.

A harlequin was standing outside the Ferenzi's palace.

"No weapons inside," he said.

I frowned and looked down at my side, then I realized his misunderstanding.

"It's not a weapon," I said, smiling, "it's a violin!" And I showed it to him.

"In that case, you're late," he said. "The musicians have already arrived."

The harlequin stood to one side and I went into the palace.

The party was being held in the reception rooms, three rooms that led one into the other with the doors open between them. The tables had been laid out in front of large marble fireplaces. At the far end was a stage where an orchestra was playing a waltz.

It was a dazzling display of luxury. The tables were draped with the finest red linen, and heaped upon them were platters of gold, piled high with all kinds of delicious food and decanters of wine. And then there were the ladies' ball gowns. Silks of all shades and colors, each design more sumptuous than the one before.

I was beginning to feel rather out of place, when suddenly I recognized the butler I had seen earlier that morning.

"Where can I find the daughter of the Count, Carla Ferenzi?" I asked him.

"How am I supposed to know? Everyone's wearing masks!" And off he went in the direction of the kitchen.

I looked around me. There were more than two hundred people and, as he said, they were all wearing masks. How could I possibly find Carla?

I was about to give up and leave the violin with one of the servants, when I had an idea. I put the instrument to my chin and began to play.

People started to gather around me; a few of them were whispering: "Who is behind the mask?"

When I had finished playing, a young woman stepped forward and asked me:

"I have never heard such a beautiful music. Who are you?"

"You wouldn't be Carla Ferenzi by any chance, would you?" I asked.

The young woman smiled. "Who knows?" she said, and melted away into the crowd.

"Are you looking for Carla?" whispered a creature, half man and half bird, that had been listening to our conversation.

"Yes. I am to present her with this violin. It is a gift from her father."

"You will find her upstairs in her room," he told me, pointing to the wide sweep of the staircase.

"You mean she's not here, at the party?"

"Carla? No. She is resting her voice. She's singing tomorrow night at the Fenice."

"Are you telling me that she is staying in her room while everyone is celebrating?"

The face behind the mask seemed to be laughing at my ignorance.

"You have obviously never heard the prima donna sing!"

34

I began climbing the stairs. On the first floor, a door to a dimly lit room had been left ajar. I peeped inside, taking care not to make a sound.

Carla was sitting in a large armchair with her eyes closed. She was only half asleep, and as soon as I entered the room, she opened her eyes. From the very first moment she looked at me I was under the spell of those eyes. They were black, and deep, and sparkling with life. Her hair, which was also black, highlighted the pale beauty of her skin, and unlike the brightly colored costumes I had seen only moments before, she was wearing a simple black velvet dress, its folds cascading softly to the floor.

She looked at me coldly and asked what I was doing in her room.

"My Lady," I heard myself saying, "I have brought the violin your father ordered for you. It is your birthday present. He asked me to give it to you, personally."

She was delighted.

"A violin? Oh, what a charming idea! I thought my father had forgotten my birthday altogether."

As soon as I heard her speak, I realized that she was the woman who had been haunting my dreams for so many years. And I also realized that I was in love with her.

I stepped forward, and taking the violin from its case, I offered it to her.

"It's very good of you to bring it," she added.

Then, lifting the violin, she asked: "May I?"

"Of course, I should be delighted."

I gave her the bow and she began playing. Her technique was somewhat limited, but her movements were graceful and flowing.

"What a wonderfully rich sound it has," she said when she stopped playing. "You are obviously a master of your craft. Unfortunately, as you can see, I am no violinist."

That may well have been the case, but it did nothing to diminish her in my eyes.

"This violin is made especially for you. I'm certain that you will soon become accustomed to it."

She played a few more notes before laying the violin down on a small table beside a wooden chessboard.

"They are beautifully carved," I said, admiring the chess pieces.

"Do you play chess?" she asked with a smile.

"I'm afraid I've never learned."

"Perhaps I could teach you," she offered.

"And in return I could teach you how to play the violin."

Still smiling, she turned toward me, watching me closely with her bright black eyes. The sounds of the party could be heard from the half-opened door.

"Does the noise not bother you?"

"Not at all," she answered. "I love the music, the songs, and the laughter. They make me happy."

"But don't you get bored up here all alone while everyone else is enjoying the party?"

"Well, what can I say? Tonight I must rest. In any case, Carnival has barely started. There'll be plenty of time after tomorrow."

"But for now you must rest your voice?"

"Did my father tell you I was a singer?"

"He did, indeed. He also told me that you have a beautiful voice. A golden voice."

"No, not at all! As it happens, I do have some slight talent as a soprano. And occasionally I sing for my friends. But tomorrow night, to celebrate my birthday, I am going to be singing at the Fenice. My father has hired out the whole theater especially for the occasion. Would you like to come along?"

I was silent for a while, trying to prolong the sheer pleasure of observing her beauty.

"My Lady, I simply can't wait to hear you sing tomorrow night. I shall most certainly be there."

"Until tomorrow night, then."

"Until tomorrow."

So we said good-bye, and after one final glance as I left the room, I went slowly down the stairs, my heart in tatters.

The party was still in full swing, but I was in no mood for it now.

35

I couldn't sleep a wink that night. I couldn't stop thinking about Carla. She was real to me now, and I could no longer pretend she was simply a dream.

First thing in the morning I went to the Ferenzi Palace. Sitting in a gondola bobbing gently on the water, I waited for some sign of life from the first-floor window, where the shutters were still closed.

In the freshness of the early dawn, the Grand Canal was covered by a light mist. Some gondoliers, carrying their goods to the market, passed me silently, gliding on the water like drifting shadows before disappearing into the labyrinth of the city.

I spent a long time staring up at that window. I was in love, the way only a person that age can be in love, uncaring of the future, and untouched by the passing of time.

That morning was the happiest moment of my entire life, waiting there secretly. Nothing else mattered. Nothing except that feeling of being in love. I had found her at last. In this strange and uncaring world, I was no longer alone.

When Carla did finally open the shutters, she was quite taken aback.

"What are you doing here?" she called out.

I was too embarrassed to tell the truth, so I said:

"I think I left my case here last night."

A few moments later she was opening the door.

"A case, you say? What kind of case?"

"The violin case."

"Ah yes, I know where it is."

She was about to go back inside looking for the case when I held her by the arm.

"Leave it," I said. "It'll be more useful to you than it is to me. Besides, I have plenty more in Cremona."

She smiled.

"Well, since you insist on being so generous . . . wait here, I'll be back in a moment."

She went back inside, and when she returned she was carrying the chessboard.

"This is for you. Last night, I saw you were admiring the chess pieces. It's never too late to learn how to play. A present, for a present!" she said, laughing.

There were a million things I would have liked to have told her. But all I did was stammer:

"Carla . . . I just wanted to say . . . you are . . ."

She put her finger gently to my lips.

"Please, don't say a word. Just take this, and go. We'll see each other again tonight at the theater."

With a ripple of laughter, she disappeared. And the mist settled once more upon the lagoon.

36

That night, Carla Ferenzi's voice was the purest of all human voices. It was the voice I had heard in my dreams.

Everyone in Venice had come to the Fenice to listen to her. Everywhere, from the stalls to the gods, people were crammed together, chatting and laughing, and occasionally breaking into song. They were all talking at once, and everyone was talking about Carla.

"They say she has the most beautiful voice in the world!"

Soon the lights went down and the theater fell silent. Slowly the curtain was raised. The orchestra started playing the opening bars of the overture. The opera had begun.

The other singers sang their parts, but by the end of the first act, the public were shouting:

"Prima donna! Prima donna!"

Everyone was waiting for Carla. She was the one they had all come to hear. She made her appearance during the second act, and as soon as she set foot on the stage, a whisper hushed the auditorium.

"Here she is!"

"It's her! It's Carla Ferenzi!"

The tension and excitement were palpable. Carla stepped forward into the light and began to sing. Immediately, everyone was entranced. The young woman's voice filled the theater.

At the end of the aria, her voice went so high, and she held the note for such a long time that for a moment, the whole audience held its breath. Nobody breathed, nobody spoke. There was a stunned silence. Then a few whispers could be heard, soon followed by a murmur of approval that turned into a roar of applause.

"Brava! Brava!"

"Viva la prima donna!"

Carla sang an encore. And the atmosphere was as magical as before.

When the curtain closed, I went straight to her dressing room.

As I opened the door she looked up, but before I'd even had a chance to speak, she said:

"Please don't say a word. Don't ever say a word about my voice. It's bad luck."

Like everyone else, I was spellbound. And she knew it.

"Do you think I made a mistake at the end? Should I have held the note a little longer?"

"You were wonderful! It was perfect!"

"Did you know that the first violin was playing your violin? He was most impressed by your craftsmanship. He asked me to pass on his compliments."

I thanked her, muttering something or other to cover my embarassment. She turned toward me, drawing a brush through her long dark hair.

"I am giving an extra performance this evening, to celebrate. Would you care to join us?"

I was too thrilled to answer.

"Don't worry, it's nothing formal. I've just invited a few friends, that's all."

"It'll be a pleasure. It's my last night in Venice, and nothing would make me happier than spending it in your company."

"That's settled then. Come to the palace at midnight, I'll be expecting you."

Smiling, she turned her head back toward the mirror. At that point, someone knocked at the door. The room was soon full of people, and Carla disappeared in a crowd of admirers.

Easing my way through the crowd, I made my way outside. I stood there in the darkness; I was overjoyed that I would be seeing her again, and yet sad because I knew it would be for the last time.

37

On the stroke of twelve, I knocked at the door. I knew Carla could never be mine, that she would always remain out of reach. I was just a humble violin-maker, and she was the daughter of the Count of Ferenzi. I was an unknown craftsman, working in the quiet of my workshop, while everyone in Venice knew who she was, and had gone to the Fenice to see her. Why, then, had fate brought the two of us together? And why did I have to fall in love with her?

The butler opened the door, and this time he recognized me.

"Her Ladyship is expecting you," he said.

I went in and, while I was taking off my coat, I heard laughter coming from the reception room. I went forward timidly.

When I saw her, she was lying on a sofa, one leg folded and the other stretched out on a cushion. Her back was straight. One of her hands was resting on the arm, while with the other she was gently running her fingers through her long black hair. Six young men were standing around her, hanging on her every word. Eventually they realized that someone else had arrived, and the talking stopped.

"Gentlemen, may I introduce you to Erasmus. He is the violin-maker I was telling you about," said Carla.

"At your service, my Lady."

Although she introduced me to everyone, I had the distinct impression that none of these gentlemen was the slightest bit interested in a lowly violin-maker, even if he had once belonged to the finest school in Cremona.

The introductions were barely over when one of them said:

"Carla was telling us that, despite your age, you are already a master violin-maker, and that the violin you made for her is a piece of great value. Is it true that you learned your art from the great Antonio Stradivari?"

"Not actually from him. Although I did learn my art in his workshop. I was apprenticed to his son, Francesco."

"Just as I thought," said another. "This violin is just like the others I saw in Cremona. You must be very grateful for the fame of your predecessors. I presume you make quite a good living by following their example."

I looked at him scornfully.

"Violin-making requires rather more than the mere ability to imitate. Each violin is different, and its quality depends on the person who makes it. So although all violins are similar, each one is unique."

"That's enough now," intervened Carla, clearly amused by our disagreement. "When will you men stop taking yourselves so seriously?"

There was a heavy silence. Then someone said:

"Carla, why don't you sing for us?"

"Yes, sing for us!"

She resisted for a while, but faced with our

insistence and feeling the need to lighten the atmosphere, she agreed.

"Very well, then. But just a short piece, because I have hardly any voice left."

So, closing her eyes, she took a deep breath, and that wonderful voice took flight once more.

Once the singing had stopped, there appeared to be some kind of competition to see who could clap the loudest.

"Well, one thing's for certain," said the arrogant individual who had addressed me previously, "no instrument in the world will ever be able to even come close to a voice like Carla's."

"Except perhaps the violin," I said. "Because the violin is the only instrument that covers the full range of the female voice, from the soprano to the contralto. And there is even something of a similarity between the female body and the shape of a violin."

"Are you trying to tell me that a woman is like a violin?"

"In a way, yes."

"Well, I must admit," said the young man, "that there are some remarkable similarities between the two. But to suggest that one could reproduce a voice—and such a voice!—with a few pieces of wood, well, that's another matter entirely."

"I'm not just suggesting it, I'm sure of it!" I said.

"That is just too much, sir."

Realizing that the conversation was in danger of turning into an argument, Carla decided to intervene. Staring at me with those beautiful eyes, she said:

"So, my dear Erasmus, would you be able to give us proof of what you are saying and reproduce the sound of my voice in one of your instruments?"

Realizing that Carla was taking his side in the argument, the young man laughed at me.

There was an uncomfortable silence, during which I was aware that everyone in the room was looking at me.

"Come on, Erasmus, please let us hear your answer," she insisted.

Perhaps it was my pride speaking, but I could think of no other way to show this woman how much I loved her. So I said:

"Carla, for you I shall make the most beautiful violin in the world. The finest violin ever made. I shall make it for you, and it will have your voice."

And little did I know that with that promise I would lose myself, and her, forever.

38

I returned home to Cremona, and began work straightaway.

The two things I remembered most vividly about Carla were the shape of her body, and the sound of her voice. So starting from these, I set out to make a violin unlike any other that had ever been made.

I ordered the finest epicea from Tyrol to make the bridge and the neck, and I chose the strongest maple, from Bohemia, for the body and side panels.

Once I had assembled the various pieces, which took several months of hard work, I coated it with a natural varnish.

Having made the violin, it took me some time to work up the courage to play it. But finally, one morning, full of trepidation, I played the first note.

It was awful. It sounded absolutely nothing like Carla's voice. I threw it to the floor in disgust.

Then I made myself a promise. A promise, which even now, I still regret:

"I swear that I shall never give up until I have made a violin that has the sound of her voice, and a color as black as her eyes."

And that was how I first had the idea of making the black violin.

39

I was standing in front of my workbench when the idea first hit me. Why not make a violin that was just like Carla? If I wanted to reproduce her voice, I should start by taking the inspiration from her body. I would have to make a violin that caught the black of her eyes and the color of her hair.

I remembered that somewhere on one of the dusty shelves in the library I had come across a small treatise, written by Antonio Stradivari himself, which explained how to make a violin made almost entirely from ebony. When I found it, I was glad to discover that among other things, the treatise contained a secret recipe for a black varnish, a varnish that I had not used before. Encouraged by my findings, I went back to work.

The shaping of the instrument's body and sound box was no simple matter. Ebony is an extremely hard wood, and to work it requires both strength and great care. Assembling all the pieces was no easy task either, but finally, after many patient hours, I succeeded. Then came the varnishing, which took me another few weeks of painstaking work.

Two months later, the black violin was finished. The last coat of varnish had dried, and the time had come to see how it sounded. That night there was a storm. The lightning lit up the sky.

I picked up the violin and ran my finger over the surface of the varnish. As I did so, the wood started singing. This was no ordinary violin.

The bow glided over the cords as gently as a feather settling on a ripple of water. The sound grew, and swelled: like a woman's voice. Like the voice of a soprano.

I stopped playing, almost bursting with happiness, for I knew I had finally made my dream come true.

That night, I played the black violin, and I played in a way I had never played any other instrument before. It was like holding Carla in my arms.

40

A few days later, I returned to Venice. It was the time they call the *acqua alta*, when the waters of the lagoon had risen and some of the tiny streets were completely flooded. And yet I felt unmoved by this sad landscape. I was so eager to see Carla again and to show her the black violin.

The Ferenzi Palace appeared to be sinking into the water of the Grand Canal. Since the quay was under water, I moored my gondola to the bars of a window. Waves rimmed with green algae were lapping at the steps.

To my surprise it was not the butler who opened the door, but Count Ferenzi himself. I was shocked by his appearance, for his cheeks were hollow, his eyes were glazed, and his skin had a waxy look to it. He had aged terribly, and seemed to be weighed down by grief.

"Ah, Erasmus," he said, "so good to see you. Perhaps you will be able to help us."

"Why, what has happened? Are you unwell?"

He took a handkerchief from his pocket and dabbed at his forehead.

"No, no. I'm fine," he said, and then, in a whisper, "it's Carla."

"Carla? What's happened to her?"

"Ah, if only I knew. She's been taken ill. She has been in bed for the last ten days."

"Can I see her?"

Without waiting for an answer, I went in and ran up the stairs. As I opened the door I saw her lying in bed, looking pale and wan. She was clearly very ill. I went over to see her.

"Carla," I whispered, "what's the matter?"

She turned her head slowly toward me and I could see from the expression in her eyes that she was in great pain.

"Look, I've brought the violin I promised you. Listen what a wonderful sound it has!"

But as soon as I touched the strings, Carla looked horrified. Her eyes widened, and she grabbed my arm, imploring me to stop.

"It's terrible," said the Count, arriving in the room behind me. "My daughter has a high fever, and the doctors have no idea what is the matter with her. The poor child has been fighting between life and death for more than a week now."

I looked at Carla, lying on the bed, her face the very picture of sadness.

"And the most terrible thing of all," said Ferenzi, "is that since the night she first became ill, she has lost her voice completely!"

I felt the ground slipping away beneath me and had to steady myself against the bedpost to stop myself from fainting.

"What's the matter?" asked Ferenzi.

"Nothing," I said. "I just feel a little tired, that's all."

I looked at Carla and could see that she was crying.

PART
THREE

41

For a while, neither of them spoke.

Then, looking at Erasmus over the rim of the glass, Johannes took a sip of grappa and they resumed their game of chess.

"Did you ever see her again?"

"Never."

"And was it because of her that you came to live in Venice?"

"It was. Although I didn't come here straight-away. As I told you, I traveled for a while. I left Cremona and went to Paris. I wanted to work, but most of all I was trying to forget the whole thing. When I finally realized I would never be able to forget, I decided to come back to Venice. But by then it was too late. It was too late for everything, then. Carla was dead."

His voice trailed off into silence, and Johannes could see that the old man had said all that he wished to say.

That night, for the first time, Erasmus lost their game of chess. It was also the first time that he had talked about himself. The first time he had really told anyone his story.

In the early hours when the game had finally come to an end, Erasmus said:

"Do you know what a magic chessboard is?"

Johannes shook his head.

"It is a chessboard on which you will never lose. Unless, that is, you betray its secret."

And with that, the old man slowly got to his feet.

"Take it," he said. "It is yours now."

42

The winter dragged on. The two men never spoke about Carla again.

One December night, Erasmus fell victim to a strange illness, and came down with a fever.

In his delirium, he whispered her name.

"Carla . . . Carla . . . Carla . . ."

Johannes sat by his bedside, watching over him, his heart going out to his old friend.

By the following day, he had lost the power of speech.

43

On the morning of the first of January 1798, Erasmus died peacefully in his sleep.

A children's choir sang at his funeral. One of the boys had an angelic voice, a voice with an air of such melancholy beauty that only the master's finest violins could have matched. And so, with the death of Erasmus, worthy successor of Antonio Stradivari, the line of great violin-makers disappeared forever.

After the ceremony in San Zaccaria, the coffin was placed on a black gondola and glided quietly along the lagoon toward the cemetery of San Michele.

It was raining that day in Venice. A fine, persistent rain. The only sounds were the rain falling on the Grand Canal, the water lapping against the sides of the gondolas, and the wind blowing among the rocks.

The funeral procession arrived at the cemetery, where Johannes watched the coffin being lowered into the ground. He scattered a handful of dark soil into the tomb, then made the sign of the cross, and hurriedly turned away.

44

Johannes went back to Erasmus's house. He wandered around, looking at the old man's meager possessions. Now and again, he'd stop to pick something up and hold it for a few moments in his hand. He sat down in front of the chessboard. For a while he just stared at the pieces, overcome with grief. Then, with a sigh, he swept them to the ground.

At that moment, he became aware of a strange humming sound. At first, he couldn't tell what it was. So he got to his feet and began to follow it. It seemed to be coming from a dark corner of the workshop. He lit a candle and went over to investigate. It was the black violin.

Johannes lifted it carefully from its hook on the wall, and then, closing his eyes, he began to play. That first note made him shiver. He was certain now this violin was cursed in some way, and would bring misfortune to anyone who played it.

But out of defiance he played it once more before flinging it to the floor in a fit of rage.

It broke as it hit the ground, and gave out a strange cry, like the cry of a woman in pain.

Johannes stumbled out into the street and ran away.

45

A few days later, Johannes left Venice with the French army and returned to Paris. He never went back to Italy.

It took him thirty-one years to compose his one and only opera. Thirty-one years in which he struggled to free himself from a voice, a dream, and the story of the black violin.

And all those years, he never played the violin again.

On the day he added the last few notes to the score of his opera, he realized that all his work had been in vain. For no one would ever be able to sing it the way Carla Ferenzi would have sung it.

And with that realization, he took the notebook on which he had been working for so long and threw it into the fire. He watched the pages blacken and curl and become engulfed in the flames. In a few moments, the work of a lifetime had disappeared.

"That's the end of that," he said to himself.

Then he lay down on his bed, exhausted but happy. For the first time in his life he was truly at peace with himself.

At long last, he had finished his imaginary opera.

He died that night in his sleep. Slipping away, quietly from the world of his dreams, to the world beyond.

And no one would ever know that he was a genius.